NEW ORLEANS SAINTS

BY JOSH ANDERSON

Published by The Child's World®
800-599-READ • www.childsworld.com

Photography Credits
Cover: © Chris Graythen / Staff / Getty Images; page 1: © Africa Studio / Shutterstock; page 3: © Grant Halverson / Stringer / Getty Images; page 5: © Edward M. Pio Roda / Stringer / Getty Images; page 6: © Jonathan Daniel / Stringer / Getty Images; page 9: © Chris Graythen / Staff / Getty Images; page 10: © Chris Graythen / Stringer / Getty Images; page 11: © stevezmina1 / Getty Images; page 12: © Jonathan Bachman / Stringer / Getty Images; page 12: © Jonathan Bachman / Stringer / Getty Images; page 13: © Chris Trotman / Staff / Getty Images; page 13: © Jonathan Bachman / Stringer / Getty Images; page 14: © Gail Oskin / Stringer / Getty Images; page 15: © Chris Graythen / Staff / Getty Images; page 16: © Streeter Lecka / Staff / Getty Images; page 16: © George Rose / Stringer / Getty Images; page 17: © Brian Bahr / Staff / Getty Images; page 17: © Mike Powell / Staff / Getty Images; page 18: © AP / Associated Press; page 18: © Brian Bahr / Staff / Getty Images; page 19: © Al Messerschmidt / Staff / Getty Images; page 19: © Chris Graythen / Staff / Getty Images; page 20: © Steph Chambers / Staff / Getty Images; page 20: © Steph Chambers / Staff / Getty Images; page 20: © Steph Chambers / Staff / Getty Images; page 21: © Sarah Stier / Staff / Getty Images; page 22: © Mike Ehrmann / Staff / Getty Images; page 23: © Donald Miralle / Staff / Getty Images; page 23: © stevezmina1 / Getty Images; page 25: © Andy Lyons / Staff / Getty Images; page 26: © Grant Halverson / Stringer / Getty Images; page 29: © Wesley Hitt / Stringer / Getty Images

ISBN Information
9781503857698 (Reinforced Library Binding)
9781503860599 (Portable Document Format)
9781503861954 (Online Multi-user eBook)
9781503863316 (Electronic Publication)

LCCN 2021952688

Printed in the United States of America

TABLE OF CONTENTS

GO SAINTS!

The New Orleans Saints compete in the National Football **League's** (NFL's) National Football Conference (NFC). They play in the NFC South **division**, along with the Atlanta Falcons, Carolina Panthers, and Tampa Bay Buccaneers. Fans in New Orleans have been lucky. The Saints have missed making the **playoffs** only five times since the 2009 season. And for 15 seasons, New Orleans was home to Drew Brees, one of the greatest quarterbacks in NFL history. Let's learn more about the Saints!

NFC SOUTH DIVISION

Atlanta Falcons

Carolina Panthers

New Orleans Saints

Tampa Bay Buccaneers

THE SAINTS WON 11 OR MORE GAMES EVERY SEASON FROM 2017 TO 2020.

SAINTS
16
PONY

BECOMING THE SAINTS

The Saints began play as an NFL **expansion team** in 1967. The team was named for a classic jazz song associated with the city of New Orleans, "When the Saints Go Marching In." While fans in New Orleans have supported the Saints since their first game, the team did not make the playoffs for their first 20 seasons. Recent years have been much better for New Orleans football. The team even won four NFC South division titles in a row from 2017 to 2020.

HALL OF FAME QUARTERBACK KEN STABLER FINISHED HIS 15-YEAR NFL CAREER WITH THE SAINTS.

BY THE NUMBERS

The Saints have won **ONE** **Super Bowl**.

NINE division titles for the Saints

547 points scored by the team in 2011—a Saints record!

13 wins for the Saints in 2019

THE SAINTS WON THE VINCE LOMBARDI TROPHY AFTER DEFEATING THE INDIANAPOLIS COLTS IN SUPER BOWL 44.

THE SAINTS HAVE WON EIGHT PLAYOFF GAMES AT THE SUPERDOME.

GAME DAY

The Saints play their home games at the Caesars Superdome in New Orleans, Louisiana. The Superdome has been the team's home since 1975, except for the 2005 season. Because New Orleans suffered such heavy damage during Hurricane Katrina that year, the Saints were forced to play their home games in other cities. The Superdome holds about 74,000 fans on game days. And the Super Bowl has been played at the Superdome seven times. That's more than any other **stadium**.

We're Famous!

The address where the Saints play their home games is on Sugar Bowl Drive. But in 2011, former Saints quarterback Drew Brees left Sugar Bowl Drive for a trip to Sesame Street. He hung out with Elmo and was a guest for the character's "Word of the Day" segment. The special word that day was *measure*. Brees used everyday items to measure Elmo, including footballs. Elmo is three footballs tall!

UNIFORM

Truly Weird

On the day the Saints drafted defensive end Cameron Jordan, something strange happened. A couple of rounds after the Saints picked Jordan with the 24th overall pick in the first round, he received a call from the Cleveland Browns informing him that *they* were drafting him. Jordan informed the Browns he'd already been picked. He then realized that the Browns meant to contact Jordan Cameron, a tight end who the Browns ended up selecting in the draft's fourth round.

Alternate Jersey

Sometimes teams wear an alternate jersey that is different from their home and away jerseys. It might be a bright color or have a unique theme. The Saints wore their special 50th anniversary uniforms for a 2016 game against the Detroit Lions. The different look proved unlucky, though. The Saints lost the game.

MOST NFL TEAMS HAVE ONLY ONE MASCOT. THE SAINTS HAVE TWO.

TEAM SPIRIT

Going to a game at the Superdome can be a lot of fun! Saints fans use the cheer "Who Dat?" as a rallying cry. After the opening coin toss, a Saints player or special guest on the field raises a hand over his or her head. When the person drops his or her hand, everyone in the Superdome launches into three ear-splitting rounds of the "Who Dat?" chant. The Saints Cheer Krewe entertains fans at every home game. The team's two mascots join them. Gumbo is a giant costumed Saint Bernard dog who wears a Saints jersey. He's joined by Sir Saint, a costumed character with a huge chin.

SIR SAINT

HEROES OF HISTORY

Marques Colston
Wide Receiver | 2006–2015

Colston played for the Saints his entire ten-year career. He gained more than 1,000 receiving yards in six of those years. His 9,759 receiving yards and 72 **touchdown** catches are the most in Saints history. He caught seven passes for 83 yards in the Saints' victory in Super Bowl 44.

Rickey Jackson
Linebacker | 1981–1993

In 2010, Jackson became the first Saints player to be inducted into the Pro Football Hall of Fame. His 40 forced fumbles rank tenth all-time, and his 136 **sacks** rank 16th. Jackson was a member of the talented "Dome Patrol" linebacker group in the late 1980s and early 1990s. He was chosen for six **Pro Bowls** in his career.

Willie Roaf

Offensive Tackle | 1993–2001

Roaf was a fixture on the Saints' offensive line for close to a decade. He was chosen for seven straight Pro Bowls from 1994 to 2000. For his career, Roaf made the Pro Bowl 11 times. He is a member of the Pro Football Hall of Fame.

The "Dome Patrol"

Linebackers | 1986–1992

Along with Rickey Jackson, linebackers Vaughan Johnson, Sam Mills, and Pat Swilling (pictured above) were nicknamed the "Dome Patrol" for their incredible defensive abilities. The four members of the Dome Patrol combined for 18 total Pro Bowl appearances during their time with the Saints. While some played longer, all four were with the team between 1986 and 1992.

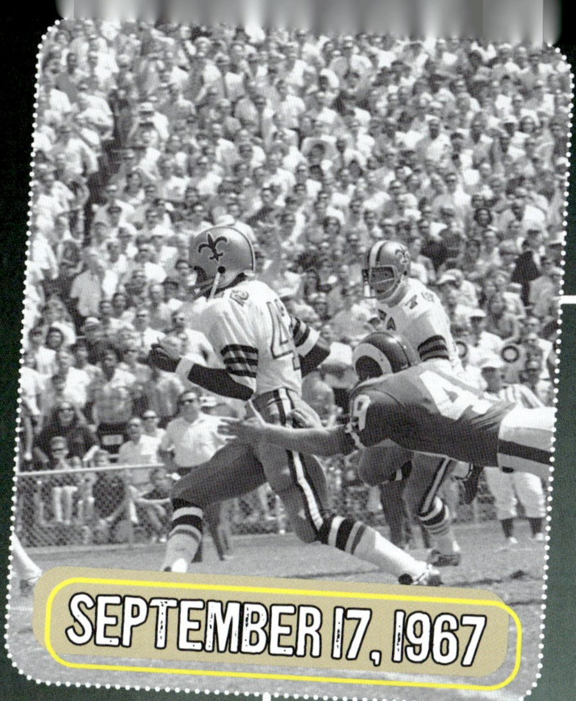

The Saints play the first game in team history, a 27–13 loss to the Los Angeles Rams.

The team earns its first playoff win ever, defeating the St. Louis Rams 31–28.

BIG DAYS

MARCH 14, 2006

After five seasons playing for the San Diego Chargers, free agent quarterback Drew Brees signs with New Orleans.

JANUARY 13, 2019

The Saints defeat the Philadelphia Eagles 20–14 to advance to the NFC Championship Game.

MODERN-DAY MARVELS

Marcus Davenport

Defensive End | Debut: 2018

Davenport played his college career at the University of Texas at San Antonio. The Saints chose him with a first-round pick in the 2018 NFL Draft. In 2021, Davenport led the Saints with three forced fumbles. He also finished second with nine sacks.

Demario Davis

Linebacker | Debut: 2018

The Saints signed Davis as a free agent in 2018. He has been an anchor for the defense ever since. He's had more than 100 combined tackles every season he's played in New Orleans. Davis was chosen as an Associated Press All-Pro after the 2019 season.

Cameron Jordan

Defensive End | Debut: 2011

Jordan has finished in the top five in the NFL in sacks three times. His 107 sacks rank second in Saints history. Jordan has started 175 of his 176 career games. He's been chosen for the Pro Bowl seven times.

Marshon Lattimore

Cornerback | Debut: 2017

Lattimore has grown into one of the league's premiere "shutdown" cornerbacks. That means he makes it very hard for the receivers he covers to get free to catch the ball. He's the only cornerback in Saints history to be chosen for the Pro Bowl four different times.

IN HIS 15-YEAR CAREER WITH THE SAINTS, DREW BREES LOGGED 142 REGULAR SEASON VICTORIES.

THE GOAT

GREATEST OF ALL TIME

DREW BREES

Brees signed with the Saints as a free agent in 2006 and led them to nine playoff appearances during his 15 years with the team. He also quarterbacked the team to victory over the Indianapolis Colts in Super Bowl 44. Brees ranks second in NFL history with 80,358 passing yards. He also ranks second all-time in passing touchdowns with 571. He was chosen for 13 Pro Bowls during his career.

#1

FAN FAVORITE

Deuce McAllister–Running Back

2001–2008

McAllister earned the love of Saints fans for his punishing, reckless running style. He used his body to help the team get every last yard. For his efforts, McAllister was chosen for the Pro Bowl twice in his career. His 1,641 rushing yards in 2003 was fourth highest in the league that season.

THE BIG GAME

FEBRUARY 7, 2010 – SUPER BOWL 44

Despite existing as a team for nearly the entire Super Bowl era, the Saints had never played in the big game until Super Bowl 44. They trailed the Indianapolis Colts late in the fourth quarter. It looked like the Saints would come out on the losing end of their first trip to the Super Bowl. But then, quarterback Drew Brees threw a touchdown pass to tight end Jeremy Shockey to give the Saints the lead. With only a few minutes remaining, cornerback Tracy Porter sealed the victory with a long interception return for a touchdown. The Saints won their first Super Bowl 31–17.

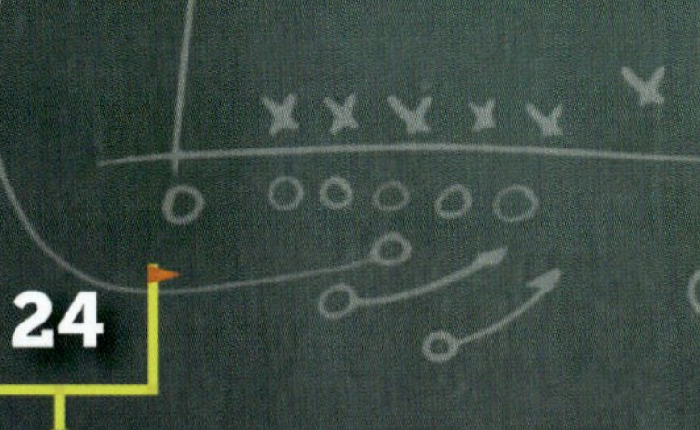

DREW BREES COMPLETED 32 OF HIS 39 PASSING ATTEMPTS IN SUPER BOWL 44.

SEAN PAYTON HAS LED THE SAINTS TO 152 VICTORIES SINCE BECOMING THE TEAM'S HEAD COACH IN 2006.

AMAZING FEATS

46
Touchdown Passes

In 2011 by
QUARTERBACK
Drew Brees

1,674
Rushing Yards

In 1981 by
RUNNING BACK
George Rogers

16
Rushing Touchdowns

In 2020 by
RUNNING BACK
Alvin Kamara

1,725
Receiving Yards

In 2019 by
WIDE RECEIVER
Michael Thomas

ALL-TIME BEST

PASSING YARDS

Drew Brees
68,010

Archie Manning
21,734

Aaron Brooks
19,156

RUSHING YARDS

Mark Ingram
6,267

Deuce McAllister
6,096

George Rogers
4,267

RECEIVING YARDS

Marques Colston
9,759

Eric Martin
7,854

Joe Horn
7,622

SACKS**

Rickey Jackson
123

Cameron Jordan
107*

Wayne Martin
82.5

SCORING

Morten Andersen
1,318

John Carney
768

Will Lutz
679

INTERCEPTIONS

Dave Waymer
37

Tom Myers
36

Sammy Knight
28

*as of 2021
**unofficial before 1982

RUNNING BACK MARK INGRAM PLAYED EIGHT SEASONS FOR THE SAINTS, FROM 2011 TO 2018, AND THEN RETURNED TO NEW ORLEANS IN 2021 AFTER TWO FULL SEASONS WITH THE BALTIMORE RAVENS.

GLOSSARY

division (dih-VIZSH-un): a group of teams within the NFL who play each other more frequently and compete for the best record

expansion team (ek-SPAN-shun TEEM): a new team added to the league

Hall of Fame (HAHL of FAYM): a museum in Canton, Ohio, that honors the best players in NFL history

league (LEEG): an organization of sports teams that compete against each other

playoffs (PLAY-ahfs): a series of games after the regular season that decides which two teams play in the Super Bowl

Pro Bowl (PRO BOWL): the NFL's All-Star game where the best players in the league compete

sack (SAK): when a quarterback is tackled behind the line of scrimmage before he can throw the ball

stadium (STAY-dee-uhm): a building with a field and seats for fans where teams play

Super Bowl (SOO-puhr BOWL): the championship game of the NFL, played between the winners of the AFC and the NFC

touchdown (TUTCH-down): a play in which the ball is brought into the other team's end zone, resulting in six points

FIND OUT MORE

IN THE LIBRARY

Bulgar, Beth and Mark Bechtel. *My First Book of Football.* New York, NY: Time Inc. Books, 2015.

Jacobs, Greg. *The Everything Kids' Football Book, 7th Edition*. Avon, MA: Adams Media, 2021.

Sports Illustrated Kids. *The Greatest Football Teams of All Time*. New York, NY: Time Inc. Books, 2018.

Wyner, Zach. *New Orleans Saints*. New York, NY: AV2 Books, 2020.

ON THE WEB

Visit our website for links about the New Orleans Saints:
childsworld.com/links

Note to parents, teachers, and librarians: We routinely verify our web links to make sure they are safe and active sites. Encourage your readers to check them out!

INDEX

ABOUT THE AUTHOR

Josh Anderson has published over 50 books for children and young adults. His two boys are the greatest joys in his life. Hobbies include coaching his sons in youth basketball, no-holds-barred games of Apples to Apples, and taking long family walks. His favorite NFL team is a secret he'll never share!